A Templar Book

Produced by The Templar Company plc,
Pippbrook Mill, London Road, Dorking, Surrey RH4 1JE, Great Britain.
Text copyright © *Redcap and the Broomstick Witch* 1926
by Darrell Waters Limited
Illustration and design copyright © 1995 by The Templar Company plc
Enid Blyton's signature mark is a registered trademark of Darrell Waters Limited

This edition produced for Parragon Books,
Unit 13-17, Avonbridge Trading Estate, Atlantic Road, Avonmouth, Bristol BS11 9QD

This book contains material first published in
The Teacher's Treasury 1926.

Illustrated by Kim Raymond and Andrew Grey

Printed and bound in Italy

ISBN 1-85813-618-0

Enid Blyton's

POCKET LIBRARY

REDCAP AND THE BROOMSTICK WITCH

Illustrated by Kim Raymond and Andrew Grey

‖ •PARRAGON• ‖

There was once a little gnome called Redcap, who lived right in the middle of Cuckoo Wood. His cottage was the cosiest little place, surrounded by trees and wild flowers. Redcap thought he was the luckiest little gnome in the world.

Early one morning he rang the little bell up on his roof to wake his friends for breakfast. Out of their holes peeped the bunnies. Squirrels scampered down from the trees.

The blackbirds and starlings came, and the robins and sparrows flew round, whistling and chirping.

Redcap gave them crumbs to eat and water to drink. He picked two of his finest lettuces for the bunnies, and gave the squirrels some nuts.

Then they sat in a ring and told each other the dreams they had had in the night.

When it came to Redcap's turn, he looked rather upset.

"I had a *horrid* dream last night," he said. "All about the Broomstick Witch. I dreamt I was taken prisoner, and I couldn't escape!"

"Never mind," said Spindly, the starling. "It was only a dream. It won't come true, Redcap. The Broomstick Witch wouldn't *dare* to come here."

"And if she did trap you," said Perky, "we'd rescue you somehow."

Redcap felt better. After all, it

was only a dream. He decided not to worry about it any more.

He ate breakfast with his friends, and soon forgot about the dream.

Later, Redcap was cooking dinner, when he heard someone walking through the wood calling out:

"Brooms for sale! Brooms for sale! Nice new brooms for sale!"

He peeped out of his window and saw an old woman with a shawl, walking up the path to his cottage.

Redcap remembered his dream. Perhaps this was the witch. Oh dear, oh dear!

"Never mind!" he thought. "She can't harm me here. Anyway, she doesn't look like a witch."

The old woman stopped at his window. "Would you like a nice new broom?" she asked.

"No, thank you," answered Redcap, though it wasn't *quite* the truth, for he did need a new broom,

He didn't want to buy one from an old woman who might be a witch though. You never knew what spell she might leave behind.

The old woman sighed, and put
the brooms over her shoulder
again. Then she sniffed at the smell
of Redcap's soup.

"Oh!" she said. "How delicious
that smells! I am so hungry, and
I've sold no brooms today."

"Well," thought Redcap, "it can't
do any harm to give her some
soup." He called her inside.

When she had eaten her meal,
the old woman thanked Redcap,

got up, and went on her way with her load of broomsticks. Later, when Redcap went outside he stared in astonishment – for leaning against his gate was a brand new broom!

Redcap took it and swept his garden path. It was a fine broom, and swept as clean as could be.

"Perky! Spindly! Bobtail!" called Redcap joyfully. "Come and see what I've got!"

All his friends gathered round.

"Where did you get it?" asked Perky. "From the old witch woman?"

"She can't be an old witch woman," said Redcap, "or she wouldn't have been so kind as to give me a fine new broom in return for the bowl of soup I gave her."

"I didn't like her," said Perky.

"Nor did we," said the others.

"Don't be silly!" laughed Redcap. "See what a fine broom it is, and see how well it sweeps!"

He began to sweep his path again – but oh dear! What do you think happened?

The broom suddenly rose in the air and *flew away with Redcap*!

"Oh!" he cried. "It's magic! It's taking me to the Broomstick Witch!"

"Perky! Climb to the tree-tops and follow him!" called Bobtail to the little squirrel. Perky leapt into the nearest tree, and soon was lost from sight.

"I *knew* she was a horrid old woman!" sighed Bobtail. "Poor Redcap! Whatever can we do?"

"We must wait until Perky comes back," said Spindly. So they waited, feeling very worried.

After a whole hour had gone by, Perky returned, out of breath.

"I followed the broom!" he panted, "and I've never travelled so fast in my life! It's gone to Red Chimney Cottage on Witchy Hill. It flew down to the garden, and as soon as it touched the ground, that old witch-woman came out and tied poor Redcap up. Then she took him indoors and I came back here!"

"Dear, dear!" said Bobtail. "We must rescue him. We promised we would if anything happened to him."

"Let's go and hide near Red Chimney Cottage," said Spindly. "We might find some way to save him tonight, when the witch is out."

So when the sun had set the little band of birds and bunnies set out, guided by Perky, who knew the way.

At last
they arrived at
Witchy Hill, and
in the darkness
crept up towards
Red Chimney Cottage.
They hid themselves carefully
beneath cabbage leaves and waited.
After a while the cottage door opened and
the witch came out. She locked the door
and put the key in her pocket. Then she
jumped on her broomstick and rode off.

Quickly Redcap's friends ran out
from their hiding places and went
up to the cottage door.

"Redcap! Redcap!" called Perky.
"Are you in there?"

"Yes!" answered Redcap. "Oh! I *am* so glad to hear you. The witch has tied me up to keep me prisoner. She wants me to help her with her bad spells, and I won't."

"Don't worry," said Bobtail. "We'll save you. We just need to find a way to get in."

They tried the door, but it was locked tight.

"Try the window!" said Redcap.

Perky jumped up on the window-sill, but there were strong bars, and no one could get in or out *that* way.

Everyone was very worried.

"We *must* do something soon, or the witch will be back!" said Perky.

"Let's all think hard!"

"I know!" cried Bobtail. "What about going down the chimney? Look, there's a tree that hangs over the roof, Perky. Couldn't you climb up, and pop down the chimney? There's no fire tonight, for the chimney isn't smoking."

"Good idea!" cried Perky, scurrying up the tree. "I'll nibble his ropes in two and Redcap will soon be free!"

In no time the little squirrel was down the chimney. He ran to where Redcap lay in a corner, tied tightly up with ropes. How glad he was to see Perky!

"Now for a good nibble!" said the squirrel, and began gnawing at the ropes as hard as he could.

One by one they fell apart, and soon Redcap was free!

"Oh! thank you, Perky," he said. "Now, how can I get out?"

He looked around in a dreadful panic, then spotted the witch's spell-book, and magic wand on the shelf. He took the big book down, put it on the table and opened it. He found the spell he needed, and turning to face the door, said:

"Abracadabra, quick as can be,
Please unlock this door for me!"
At once, the door sprang open! All his friends outside crowded round him in delight.

"Come home quickly," they said, "before the witch comes back."

"Hold on," said Redcap. "I have an idea."

He went back inside and brought out all the brooms he could find.

"Listen!" he said. "A witch is no good without her brooms. Take one each and sit on it. There are enough brooms for everyone but me."

"But we can't leave you behind, Redcap!" cried everyone.

"You won't have to!" said the gnome, chuckling. "I shall hide in the garden till the witch comes back. When she gets off *her* broom and goes inside, I shall take it quickly, say the magic rhyme, and off we'll all

go as quick
as lightning,
leaving her behind!"
"What a splendid
idea!" cried Bobtail.
"Then she'll be harmless,
and we'll all get a good
ride home. What fun!"
"Sh! Sh!" suddenly said Perky.
"She's coming! Hide quickly!"
They took the broomsticks
to the long grass. Redcap hid

among some hollyhocks near the door, and waited.

Down flew the witch on her broomstick, and landed by the door.

She jumped off and leaned it up against the wall just near Redcap. Then she felt in her pocket to find the key. At the same moment Redcap gave a tremendous yell, snatched the broom and jumped on it. His friends did the same, and the witch fell over backwards in fright.

"Broomstick, fly
Away to the sky;
High and then low,
Away we go!"
As Redcap sang these magic
words the broomsticks rose in the
air and flew to Cuckoo Wood. The
old witch called them, but they
wouldn't go back to *her* any more!

When the friends arrived home
after a fine ride, they chuckled in
delight to know their little friend

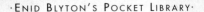

was safe once more. Redcap
thanked them again and again.

"Now put your broomsticks in a
heap," he said, "and we'll burn them.
Then the old witch can do no
more harm!"

The broomsticks
were so full of magic
that as they burnt
the flames were
green and the
smoke was red.

Then the friends went to bed, and settled down happily to sleep, knowing they would have breakfast together in the morning, and they didn't need to worry about the Broomstick Witch any more!